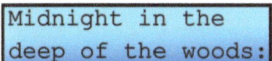

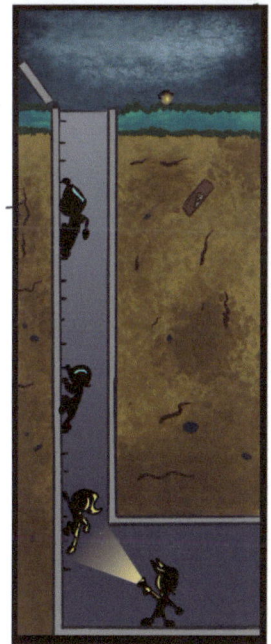

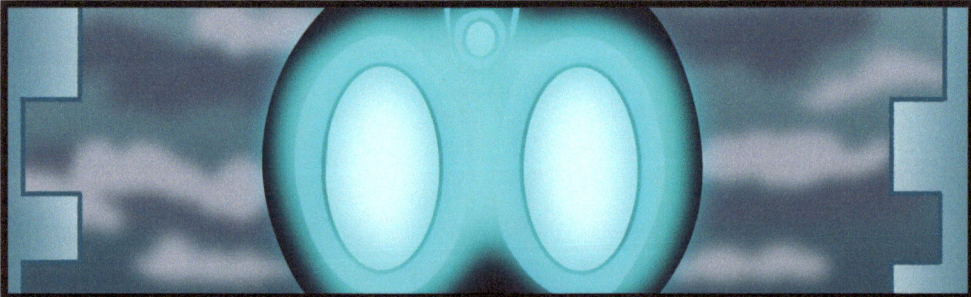

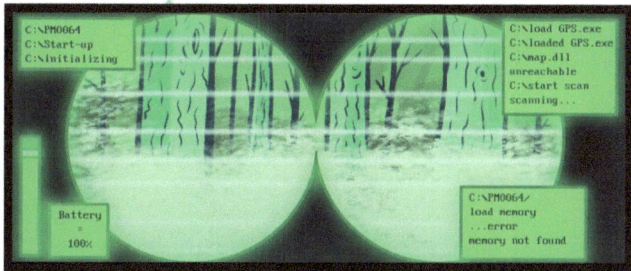

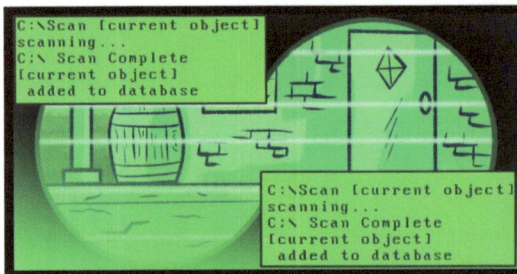

Not too far away...

What in blue blazes is this thing!

I think we done hit a kid!

This ain't no kid. This is some sorta machine— —a robut 'a some sort.

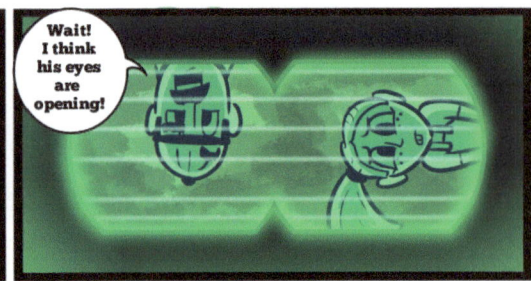

Wait! I think his eyes are opening!

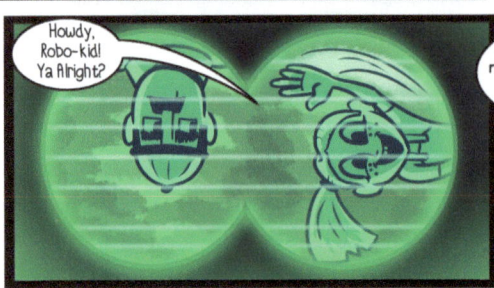

Howdy, Robo-kid! Ya Alright?

Yes, my systems are running at peak capacity, and my energy is at 98.2%.

What's your name?

Where did ja come from?

I am project model #00064, and I awoke approximately ten hours and fifty-seven minutes ago somewhere I have no memory of.

He's amazin'! Can we keep 'im, Pa!

PLEASE!?!?

Ya said I couldn't get a dog, so can I get a robot instead? He won't make a mess in the cab!

Buck, a dog is one thing, but a robut is another. Heavens to Betsy—

I'm still havin' a hard time believin' he's real! Besides we got no room for 'im.

'Course we do, Pa! We can shove 'im in the passenger seat, and I'll sit in the cargo hammock. 'Sides, we can't just leave him out here on the highway!

Scratch

Scratch

Just look at the poor boy! He don't know what he's doin'. We could help 'im out!

Did it ever occur to ya, Buck, that maybe he belongs to somebodies else?

Or that he might not want to go for a ride?

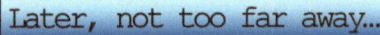

Ah'm tellin' you! It was some sort of alien or robot! Yes, I called F.I.S.T.

they told me they were sending someone.

Sheriff Avery J. Cletus? I'm agent 187.

I was sent here to interrogate your suspect.

Right! A pleasure ta meetcha!

Some kid came in here and told me he knows where the dem thing came from.

You were correct to inform us first. I will need to have a word with you when I am finished.

Where did you find the robot?

Geez, man, who are you? Some kinda G-man?

I am F.I.S.T. Agent 187. Department of Techno-Security. My superiors have a great interest in procuring the target —this robot which you speak of.

Now, I repeat my question —this time, you answer me.

F.I.S.T

Where did you find the robot?

Umm... well, we-me and my friends- found this hatch in the woods last night, and it led down to this really spooky lab. That's where we saw it!

Geez, man, we aren't in trouble, are we?

Not at the current moment.

This laboratory

—this hatch

—I need you to take me there.

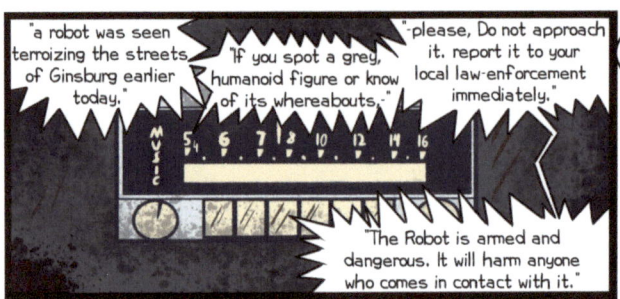

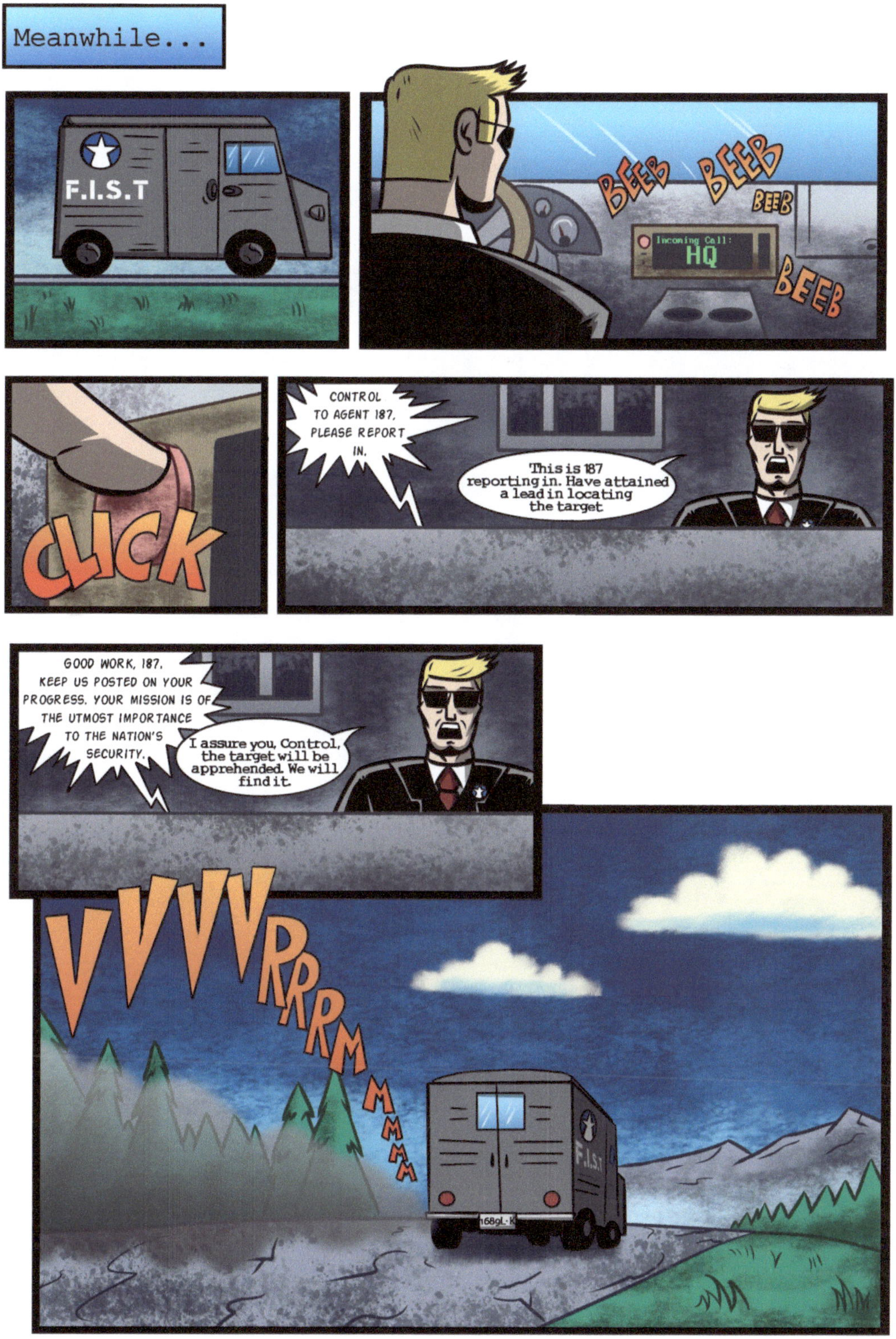

Meanwhile...

CONTROL TO AGENT 187, PLEASE REPORT IN.

This is 187 reporting in. Have attained a lead in locating the target

GOOD WORK, 187. KEEP US POSTED ON YOUR PROGRESS. YOUR MISSION IS OF THE UTMOST IMPORTANCE TO THE NATION'S SECURITY.

I assure you, Control, the target will be apprehended. We will find it.

Now, repeat to me at least three contractions and their combined words.

Awright! Umm... "Could not" is "Couldn't." "Should not" is "shouldn't"–

–And "am not" is "ain't."

According to my language data-base, "ain't" is not a correct contraction.

Well, your data-base must be real old, because everybody uses 'ain't' nowadays.

Hmm, it does seem to increase the efficiency of communication...

I will add it to my lexicon, then.

He's supposed to be teachin' you, Buck–

–not the other way around.

I am programmed with a capability to speak your language with access to all the words in the Freeland Standard Dictionary volume 14 and guided by Melton's Standard Grammar volume 3.

You sure know a lot about grammar, where didja learn all this stuff, anyhow?

Wow! You got a whole encyclomapedia in your computers, too?"

Unfortunately, while I can communicate and carry out simple tasks, I do not have access to further information.

Yet, I am capable of absorbing, examining, and compiling new information every second.

Well then, if you want to learn tons a' stuff, there's no better place than the open road!

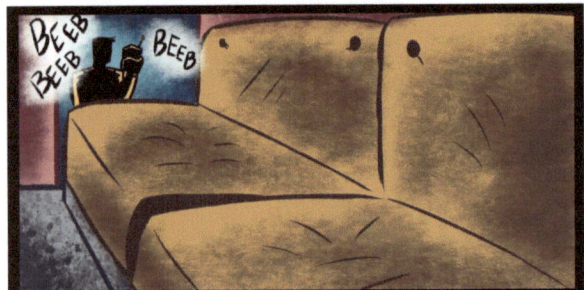

AAAAAAHHHHHHHHHHᴴᴴᴴ

Woahwoahwoah. Stop that now, y'hear?

I do not understand. You said that screaming is expected when one enjoys a ride.

Naw! Ya don't scream on slow rides, only fast ones.

Well, Power Boy, its been fun, but we should probably head back to the rig after this.

Bucky, do you see that man over there? The one with the black suit and sunglasses.

Yeah?

BEEB BEEB BEEB BEEB BEEB

Over all the other people, he continues to show up the most—particularly behind us. It is possible that he might be following us.

Darn... you might just be right. And we can't lead him back to the truck...

See that junkyard over there? We'll give him the slip here, head on over there, then double back to the truck. Waddaya say?"

I do not understand what a piece of paper has to do with anything, but this maneuver seems logical.

A few hours later...

SIMPLY FASCINATING!

Do ya think you can fix him?

WELL, I HAVE BEEN EXAMINING HIS BODY FOR PORTS OF ACCESS, BUT CANNOT FIND A SINGLE ONE—SAVE FOR THE CHARGING PORT ON HIS BACK.

IT'S REALLY QUITE FASCINATING, EVERY TIME I PRY AT ONE OF HIS JOINTS, MY TOOL IS REPELLED.

THERE'S A SORT OF MICROSCOPICALLY THIN ENERGY FIELD WHICH KEEPS HIM TOGETHER. I DOUBT I'LL BE ABLE TO GAIN ANY SORT OF ACCESS TO HIS SYSTEMS.

TAPTAP

OH! UMM....

DON'T FRET! I MAY STILL BE ABLE TO WORK SOMETHING OUT.

You said that outlet on his back is a "chargin' port?" Of some kind?

INLET.

A POWER OUTLET DISTRIBUTES ELECTRICAL ENERGY—INSTEAD OF COLLECTING IT. AND, YES, IT IS. IT IS UNLIKE ANY STANDARD TYPE I HAVE EVER SEEN.

YOU... WOULDN'T HAPPEN TO HAVE THE ADAPTER AND CHARGING APPARATUS WHICH GOES WITH HIM, WOULD YOU?

'Fraid not. Ran smack-dab into him while on the road. Said he didn't know who made him or where he was from —only that he woke up in some abandoned lab underground.

FASCINATING... HIS INTEGRITY WITHSTOOD A HEAD-ON COLLISION WITH A SEMI-TRUCK?

Sure did.

Do you know who built Power Boy?

WELL, I... JUST CURIOUS, BUT WHY IS HE CALLED POWER BOY?

It's his name! Picked it out himself, he did!

POWER BOY IS UNLIKE ANY PIECE OF TECHNOLOGY I HAVE EVER EXAMINED. FOR OVER THIRTY YEARS NOW, THE DEVELOPMENT OF ROBOTS AND ARTIFICIAL INTELLIGENCE HAS BEEN HALTED BY STRICT GOVERNMENT INTERVENTION.

Now, why's that?

YEARS AGO, WHEN YOUR FATHER WAS ONLY A BOY AND I WAS IN MY YOUTH, ROBOTIC DRONES WERE DEVELOPED BY PROFESSOR JOSHUA KYRIE —THE CHIEF SCIENTIST OF DEUS LABS.

THESE ROBOTS HELPED THE PUBLIC AT LARGE. THEY AIDED PEOPLE IN BUSINESS, TRANSPORTATION, HAZARDOUS WORK, AND MANY OTHER AREAS.

KYRIE WANTED TO GO A STEP FURTHER AND CREATE A SORT OF MASTER-DRONE TO GOVERN OVER THE OPERATIONS OF THE REST.

THIS ROBOT WAS KNOWN AS PARAGON,

AND KYRIE GAVE HIM ARTIFICIAL INTELLIGENCE SO ADVANCED THAT IT WAS SAID TO BE ABLE TO THINK AND FEEL ALL ON ITS OWN.

ONE DAY, THE WORLD WATCHED IN HORROR AS PARAGON TRIED TO COMMAND THE DRONES AS AN ARMY TO OVERTHROW FREELAND AND DESTROY KYRIE.

SOMEHOW, KYRIE MANAGED TO SHUT DOWN THE DRONES AND DESTROY PARAGON.

HE THEN DISAPPEARED —NEVER TO BE SEEN AGAIN.

FROM THAT DAY FORWARD, ROBOTICS AND ALL SCIENTIFIC RESEARCH ASSOCIATED WITH THE FIELD WERE RESTRICTED OR HEAVILY MONITORED AT LEAST TO PREVENT THE CHAOS AND DESTRUCTION THAT OCCURRED ALL THOSE YEARS AGO.

KYRIE— —ONE OF THE MOST BRILLIANT MINDS THE WORLD HAD EVER SEEN— —IS STILL WANTED BY THE GOVERNMENT TO THIS DAY

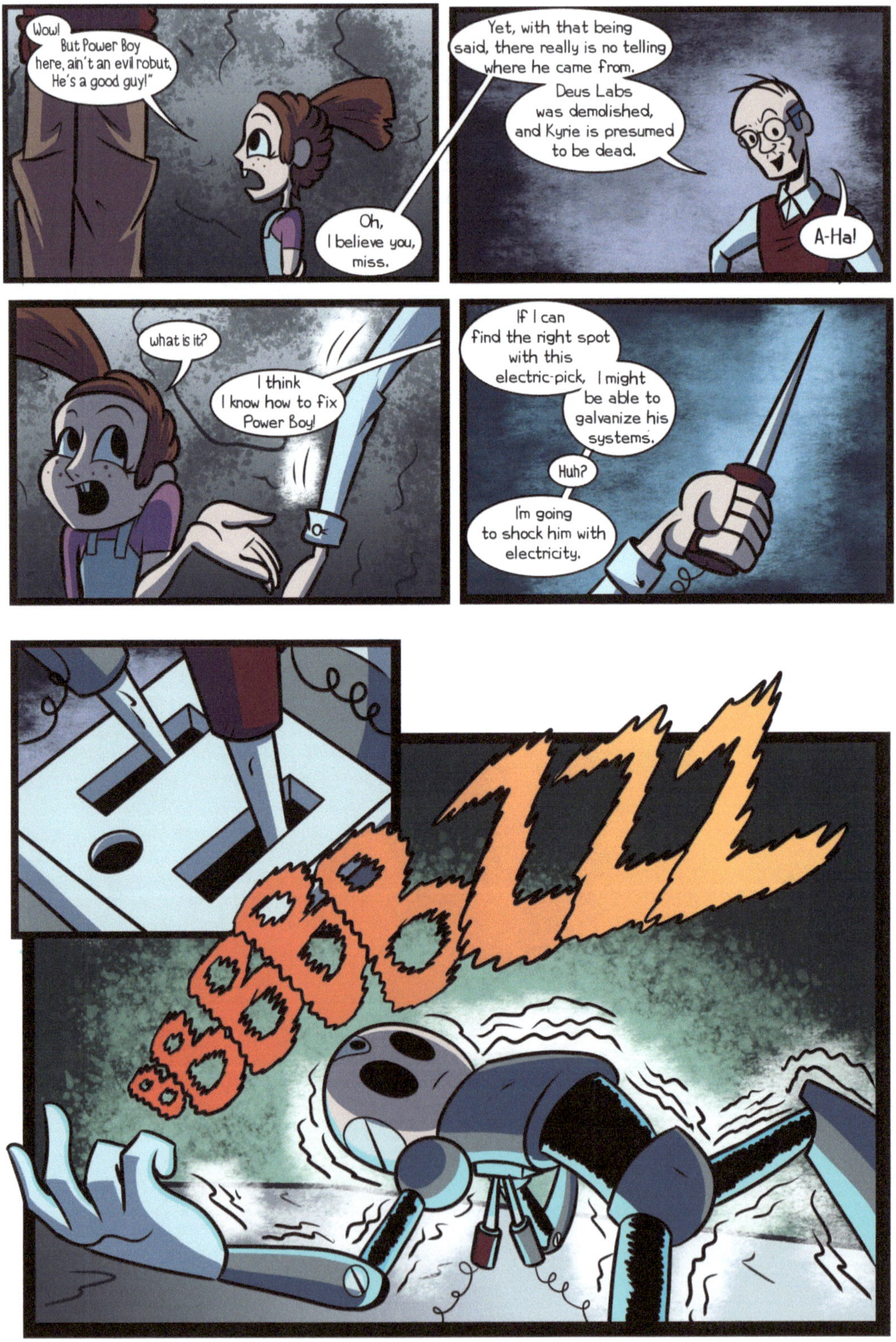

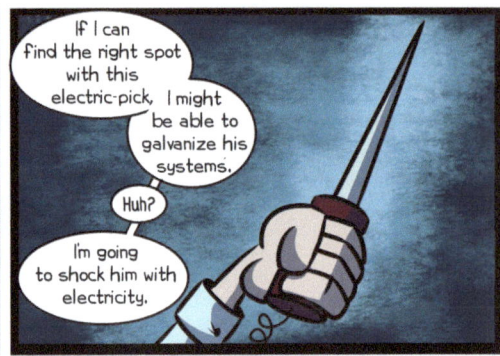

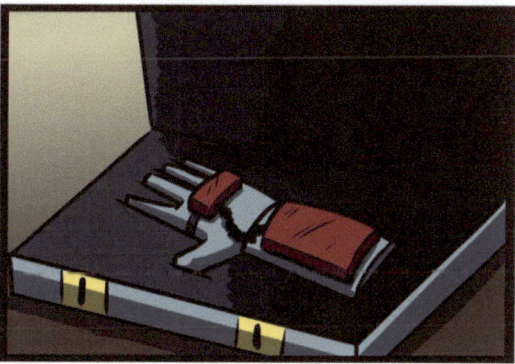

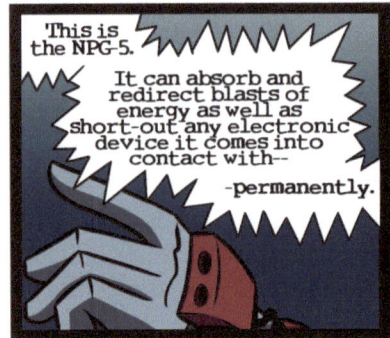

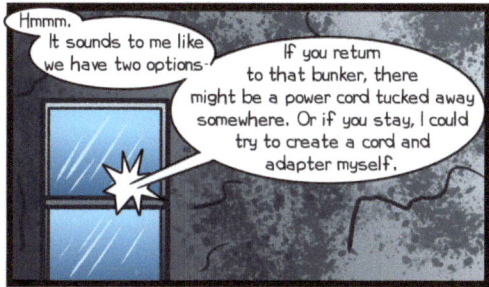

Hmmm. It sounds to me like we have two options-

If you return to that bunker, there might be a power cord tucked away somewhere. Or if you stay, I could try to create a cord and adapter myself.

However, this would be incredibly tricky, and it would take some time-there's no guarantee I can make one. Whoever created you, it seems they really wanted to ensure that no outside influence could access your systems

Power Boy, do you know how much more juice you have?

I am at 35% and dropping. Taking account of the energy I've expended as well as the time I have spent online,

I calculate that I have 2 days, 3 hours, and 21 minutes left of battery life.

And less time if I use my laser-beam.

What?!?

We ain't gonna let you die for real! Pa, we can do somethin', right?

It's your choice what ya want to do, son.

Thank you for your offer of letting me stay with you, Professor. It is the most reasonable choice for solving my problem.

However, if my time is limited and there is no guarantee that I will be able to be brought back online, I would prefer to spend the remainder of my time in the company of my friends.

Are ya certain about this, now?

They'll still be lookin' for ya over at Ginsburg.

Most likely. Which is why I will now ask that you both accompany me no further than the town border. I do not wish to put you and/or Bucky in harm's way.

You can't, Power Boy! What if ya find a power cord in that bunker and get re-charged?

My presence seems to put you and your father in danger. It would be more logical to continue my search alone.

Then, I will continue to search for my creator.

recent events have caused me to re-evaluate my approach.

But, Power Boy! Ya can't leave us! Why would ya want to leave us?

I have... come to care for the both of you.

And it is because I care that I wish to ensure your safety.

Pa! Tell him he don't have to go! You can lick anyone who messes with us—

—ain't that right, Pa?

It's what he needs to do, Buck.

And sometimes, a man's gotta do what a man's gotta do.

But what if ya don't find a power cord? What if ya run out of juice?

If that were to happen, then I would prefer to lose consciousness in the place where I was found—

Ya can't leave, Power Boy! You're the bestest friend I ever had!

—in hope that my creator might return and find me.

And you, Bucky are my 'bestest friend' as well. You and Pa are the 'bestest friends' I have made on this trip.

The last thing I would want is to see either of you come to any harm.

After dropping off 16,000 Capperdams...

Next stop, Ginsburg—

—with a haul of one, whole Power Boy

Yeah, they just left. Said they was head-ing to Ginsburg.

Click

Wha-?

Hello?

Well, son, I just wanted to tell ya ...I'm proud of you for making such a tough call,

and mighty glad you chose to ride with us.

I'm half-tempted to ask ya to stay on with us— if only to keep teachin' Bucky.

It has been an interesting journey, Pa.

Thank you again, for taking me to Sandburg and back.

S'no problem. Listen, if we are gonna make it to Ginsburg as quick as possible, I'm gonna need some sleep.

I'm gonna stop at a motel, we'll catch a few hours of shut-eye, then we'll head on over to Ginsburg first thing in the mornin'.

That alright?

Sounds reasonable.

The STAR DEAL MOTEL

BEEB

Well... when I tell Bucky to do something, it's to protect her—

—it's for her own good.

Now, the government, they don't know you.

BEEB

They think you're some kinda threat, when you're just a good-hearted kid.

BEEB

I get the impression they want to see you destroyed, and that ain't for your own good at all.

BEEB

BEEB

Ya see, I didn't always have Bucky in the cab to keep me company.

BEEB

BEEB

I used to make my hauls across Freeland on my own...

...and I typically made better time.

BEEB

BEEB

BEEB

But back home, Buck was... bein' brought up in a bad way.

BEEB

I didn't want to see no harm come to Buck, so I brought her along.

BEEB

It's been tough—

BEEB

Raising a child on the road—but it's for her own good.

BEEB

Now, keepin' Bucky with me ain't exactly legal, either, but like you, the government don't know what's best for her.

BEEB

You understand?

I suppose I...

BEEB

BEEB

Wait...

BEEB

That beeping noise. That is the sound of—

BEEB BEEB

BEEB BEEB

BEEB BEEB
BEEB BEEB
BEEB BEEB
BEEB BEEB

BEEB BEEB
BEEB BEEB
BEEB BEEB
BEEB BEEB
BEEB BEEB

CRASH

PM 0064, my son-
my name is Joshua Kyrie: your creator. This message should play moments after you have come online; if not, I fear you have been activated prematurely.

You were built with something which no other machine possesses- autonomy: the ability to think for yourself.

I built you for the purpose of protecting all humans. You do not mechanically follow directions, but are able to determine your actions for yourself. You have the freedom to choose between good and evil.

Your older brother had this same gift, yet he chose to use that gift as a way of terrorizing others and making himself great.

I know you must have many questions but now, it is important that you make your way to Flint City's eastern docks as quickly as possible.

I will be waiting there for you.

C:/PM0064 is now active
retreiving GPS
Location...

My child-
-He lives!

That was Awesome!

Anyone want to do that again?

No!

No!

No!

Daggumit! It looks like we're bein' followed!

It's the G-man!

Shoot! I thought tying him up would have bought us a little more time!

That man's as stubborn as an oak stump!

FLIP

TAK TAK TAK

I got an idea.

SKREEEEEE

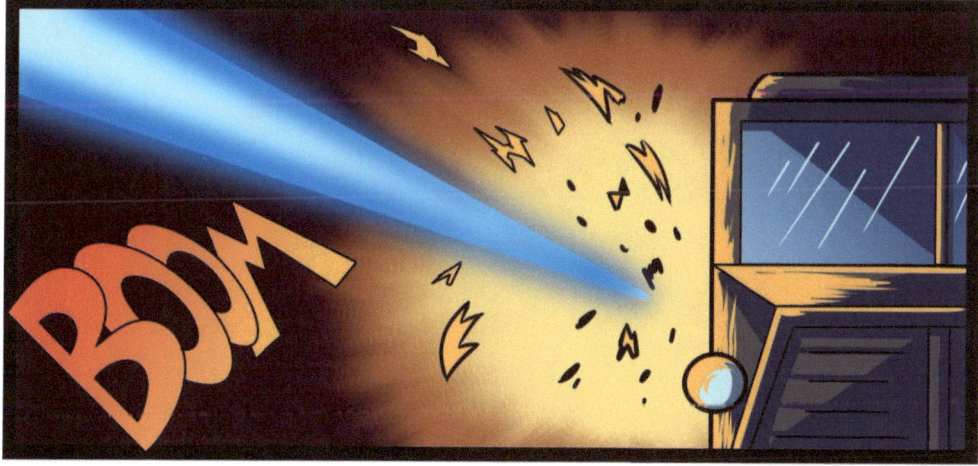

Whooo!!!

Look up ahead!

Flint City!

Looky-there, Power Boy! We made it!

Pa, could you please pull over?

What now, son?

Pull over, Pa. Please.

I've been giving this a lot of thought, and...

I think this is where we need to part ways.

My purpose is to protect human life,

and my presence has only put you both in danger.

So, before more G-men come after me,

I kindly ask that you let me go the rest of the way on my own.

Imma miss you, Power Boy!

You're my bestest friend!

"Imma" miss you as well, Bucky.

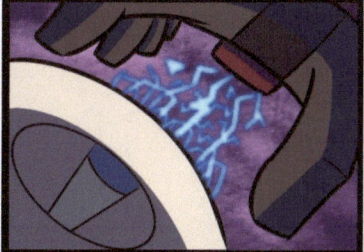

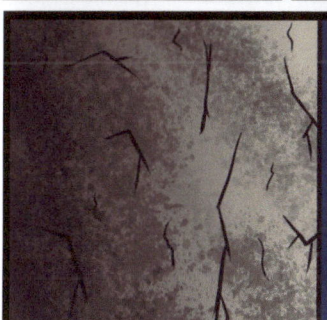

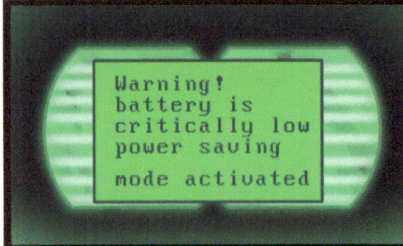

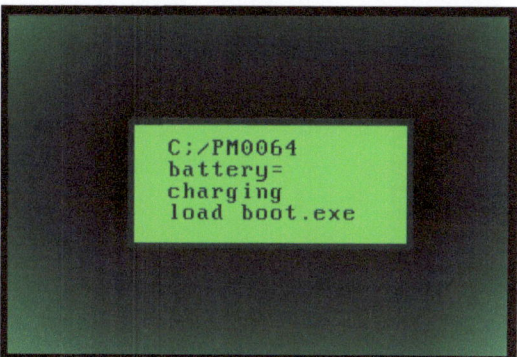

Only you can choose whether to stand up for what's right or kneel before evil.

Concept Art

Early Character Deigns

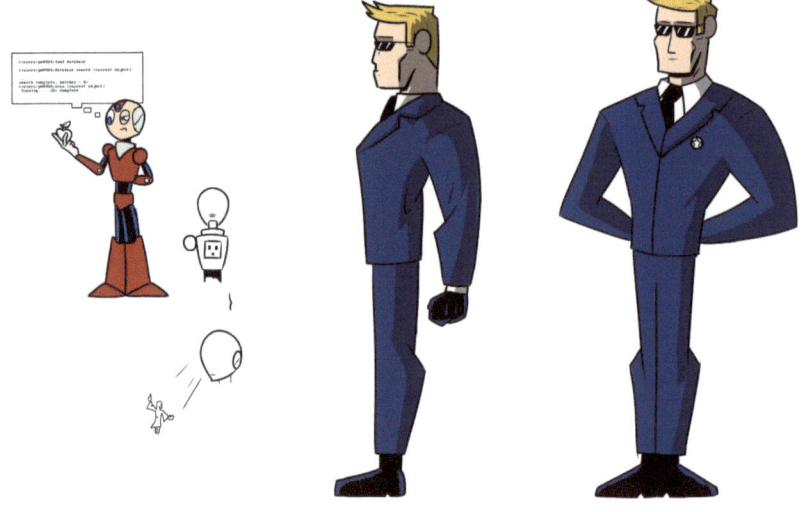

Huge thanks to my brother, David Nanney for this one piece of art (bellow) he did for this project.

Locations and Landscapes

www.ingramcontent.com/pod-product-compliance
Lightning Source LLC
Chambersburg PA
CBHW041147250626

47164CB00013B/14